To my son, Ryan, the best gift I ever received,
and in memory of his Nana, my mother—
who always made the days leading up to Christmas
the very best times of the year — T. S.

Henry Holt and Company, LLC, *Publishers since 1866*
115 West 18th Street, New York, New York 10011 [www.henryholt.com]

Henry Holt is a registered trademark of Henry Holt and Company, LLC

Distributed in Canada by H. B. Fenn and Company Ltd.

Library of Congress Cataloging-in-Publication Data
Smythe, Theresa.
Snowbear's Christmas countdown / Theresa Smythe.
Summary: During each day of the month of December, Snowbear prepares for and celebrates the Christmas season.
[1. Christmas—Fiction. 2. December—Fiction. 3. Bears—Fiction. 4. Counting—Fiction.] I. Title.
PZ7.S66493Sn 2004 [E]—dc22 2003023527

ISBN 0-8050-7244-6 / EAN 978-0-8050-7244-0 / First Edition—2004 / Designed by Amy Manzo Toth
Printed in the United States of America on acid-free paper. ∞
1 2 3 4 5 6 7 8 9 10

The artist used cut-paper collage to create the illustrations for this book.

Theresa Smythe

SNOWBEAR'S CHRISTMAS COUNTDOWN

Henry Holt and Company ❄ New York

It was the month of December and time for Snowbear to get ready for Christmas.

On the 1st day he wrote a list of all the presents he wanted Santa to bring him.

On the 2nd day he took his favorite wool hat and scarf out of the storage closet and checked them for moth holes.

On the 3rd day he strung a cord of brightly colored lights along the roof.

On the 4th day he arranged his collection of snow globes on the mantel.

On the 5th day he wrote and mailed all of his Christmas cards.

On the **6**th day he shoveled a path from his house because it had snowed the night before.

On the **7**th day he made a snowman.

gLue
gLitt

On the 8th day he made ornaments out of paper, glitter, and glue.

On the 9th day he picked out a Christmas tree and brought it home to decorate.

On the 10th day he
set up his toy trains.

On the 11th day he went Christmas shopping.

On the 12th day he wrapped all his presents for his family and friends.

On the 13th day he went sledding down the giant hill near his house.

On the 14th day he caught a cold and had to stay in bed.

On the 15th day he watched his favorite holiday movies and snuggled under the blankets.

On the **16**th day he cracked nuts with his new nutcracker.

On the 17th day he hung a wreath on his door.

On the 18th day he bought a poinsettia plant to brighten up the kitchen.

On the **19**th day he had Charlie over for lunch.

On the **20**th day he ate too many candy canes and got a bellyache.

On the 21st day he went caroling with his friends.

On the 22nd day he went ice-skating
and counted the stars.

On the 23rd day he hung up his stocking and read a book by the fire.

On the 24th day it was Christmas Eve, so he made a plate of cookies for Santa and his reindeer.

HArry
Harry
TOM
RAY
TOM

And on the **25th** day, with the help of all his friends, he had himself a very **Merry Christmas**!

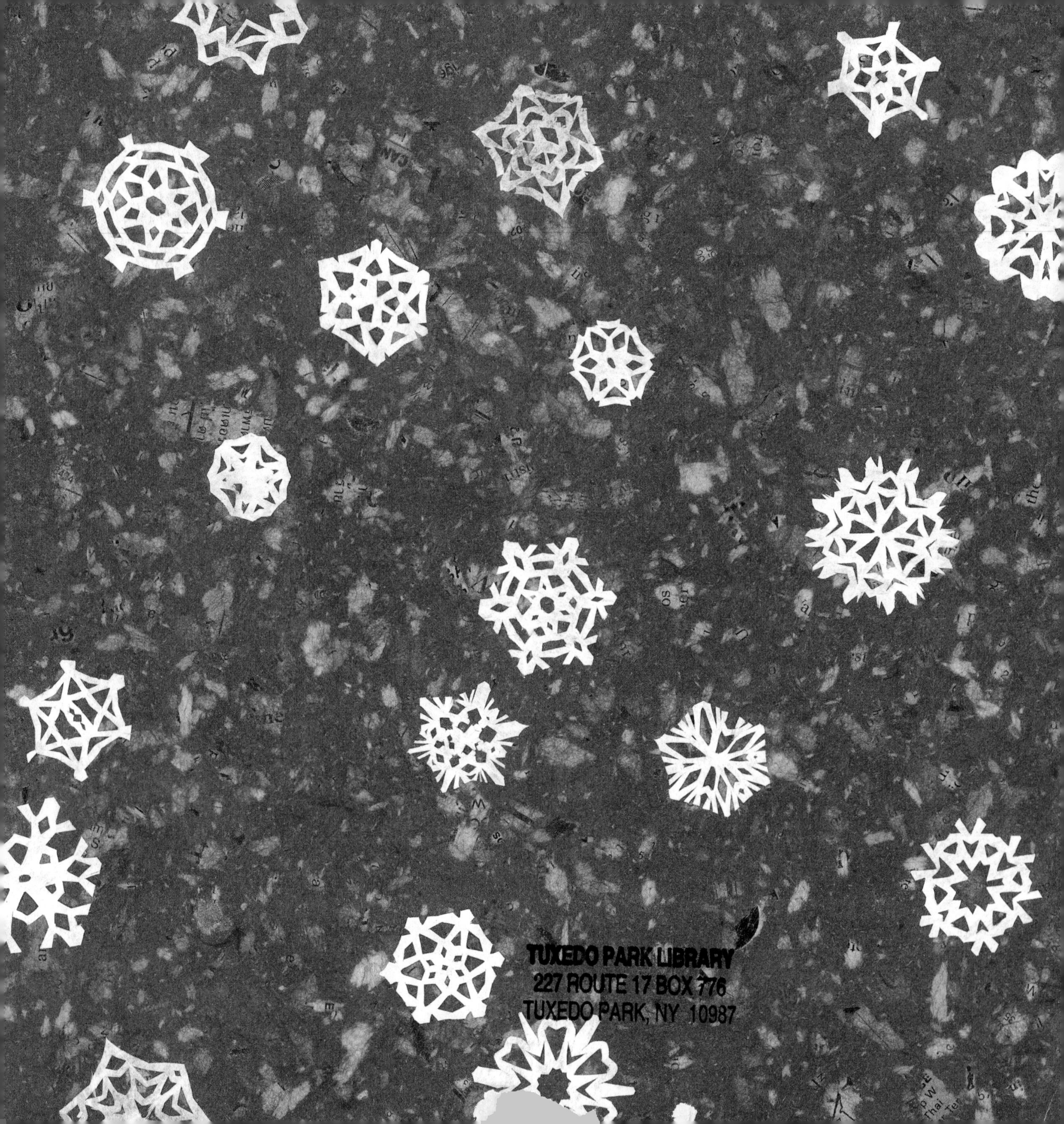